**"What is going on?"** asked Titus.

Timothy added, "What makes that one red flower near the idol so special? And why are those teenagers picking the flower up and putting it down?"

It's time for the T.C.D.C. to solve another mystery!

THE MYSTERY OF THE

# SILENT
# IDOL

*Elspeth Campbell Murphy*
*Illustrated by Chris Wold Dyrud*

*Lake Shore Baptist Church*

# Chariot Books
David C. Cook Publishing Co.

A Wise Owl Book
Published by Chariot Books,
an imprint of David C. Cook Publishing Co.
David C. Cook Publishing Co., Elgin, Illinois 60120
David C. Cook Publishing Co., Weston, Ontario

The Mystery of the Silent Idol
© 1988 by Elspeth Campbell Murphy for text and Chris Wold
Dyrud for illustrations

Cover design by Chris Patchel
First Printing, 1988
Printed in the United States of America
93 92 91          5

Library of Congress Cataloging-in-Publication Data

Murphy, Elspeth Campbell.
    The mystery of the silent idol.

    (Ten commandments mysteries)
    ''A Wise owl book''—T.p. verso.
    Summary: Three cousins uncover a drug dealing operation and
learn about the commandment, ''You shall not make yourself an
idol.''
    [1. Ten commandments—Fiction. 2. Drug abuse—Fiction. 3.
Cousins—Fiction. 4. Mystery and detective stories] I. Dyrud, Chris
Wold, ill. II. Title. III. Series: Murphy, Elspeth Campbell. Ten
commandments mysteries.
PZ7.M95316Myh   1988      [Fic]        87-24285
ISBN 1-55513-527-7

"You shall not make for yourself an idol."

*Exodus 20:4 (NIV)*

# CONTENTS

# 1
# AT THE MALL

"It's not fair!" Timothy Dawson complained to his cousin, Titus McKay, and his other cousin, Sarah-Jane Cooper. "Stores shouldn't even be *allowed* to sell back-to-school clothes in the middle of summer! School doesn't start for *ages*! So why do we have to go shopping for school clothes now? It's not fair!"

Titus and Sarah-Jane just looked at Timothy as if they couldn't think of the right thing to say. Timothy was the only one who was in a crabby mood. When it came to shopping for new clothes, Sarah-Jane loved it, Titus felt OK about it, but Timothy *hated* it.

Timothy glanced at his mother. Sure enough, she was giving him a warning look that said—almost as clearly as words—"Snap out of the crabby mood, kid!''

Timothy and his mother, plus Sarah-Jane and *her* mother (Aunt Sue), plus Titus and *his* mother (Aunt Jane) were all at the new Woodhill Mall. Timothy's baby sister had stayed home with a neighbor. "Lucky Priscilla," Timothy thought. "Just goofing off—as usual."

Sarah-Jane, who was visiting from the country, tried to cheer him up. She said, "Wow, Tim! You're so lucky to have this mall right near your house!"

"Yeah," said Titus, who was visiting from the city. "It's really EXcellent!"

That didn't make Timothy feel any better. Everybody always said how wonderful the new mall was. But Timothy never liked being there. And it made him feel kind of lonely when he didn't like something that his cousins thought was so neat-O.

Woodhill had about two hundred stores. It had flowers and trees and fountains. It even had a waterfall and a little stream with a bridge going over it. But the mall always made Timothy feel cooped up in a funny sort of way. He didn't think

10

trees and waterfalls should have a roof over them.

Timothy sighed and leaned his arms on the railing the way Titus and Sarah-Jane were doing. They looked down at the ramps and escalators and shoppers.

Suddenly Timothy spotted someone he knew and waved to him.

"Who are you waving to, Tim?" asked Titus.

"It's Jeff," said Timothy. "But he doesn't see me!"

"Who's Jeff?" asked Sarah-Jane.

"You *know*!" said Timothy. "He's that teen-ager who lives next door to me. The one who lets me hang around with him sometimes." (Timothy had never told anyone, but sometimes he liked to pretend Jeff was his big brother.)

"Oh, yeah," said Sarah-Jane. "He's really nice. But right now he looks like he's in a bad mood, too."

Timothy looked again at Jeff. The older boy was studying the mall directory. He was frown-ing hard, and he kept looking at his watch.

"Maybe he's lost," said Titus. "Maybe he's mad because he can't find the store he wants."

11

"Or maybe he just hates shopping," said Timothy. "Like me."

"But if he hates shopping, what's he doing at the mall?" asked Sarah-Jane.

"Teenagers always come to the mall," said Timothy.

"But that's because they like to wander around with their friends," said Sarah-Jane. "Jeff is all by himself—and he doesn't look like he's having a very good time."

Timothy waved again, but Jeff still didn't see him. The teenager just looked at his watch and wandered into the nearest store.

Titus said, "Maybe he's waiting for someone. Or maybe he's just killing time."

Not being able to get Jeff's attention didn't make Timothy feel any less crabby. "*Now* where are we going?" he asked his mother. He knew he sounded whiny, but he couldn't help it.

"I think you'll feel better after you eat," said his mother. She was using her I'm-being-very-patient-with-you voice. "Your aunts and I want to try this new place we've heard a lot about."

Timothy cheered up a little at the thought of a great, big, cheesy pizza—or maybe a hot dog or a hamburger.

But when they got to the restaurant, Timothy was shocked. He couldn't believe his eyes.

It was some new, fancy-looking place called *Tropical Gardens*.

It was decorated all around the outside with

palm trees and big, brightly colored, artificial flowers. Over the front door there was a picture of an old-time sailing ship. And around the side of the restaurant—facing a quiet corner of the mall—there were plants and flowers and a funny-looking statue.

Timothy peeked inside the front door. There were basket chairs and lamps in the shape of sea-shells.

"I hate this restaurant!" Timothy said.

"How do you know you hate it?" cried his mother. "You've never even been here before!"

"That doesn't matter," Timothy said. "I can still tell what kind of a restaurant this is. It's the kind of place where they put pineapple and coco-nut on everything. Pineapple is bad enough! But coconut is pukey! Bleah! Bleah!"

Timothy's mother looked like she was getting ready to say, "Young man, do you have to go sit in the car?"

But Titus came to the rescue. "It's OK, Tim!" he said quickly. "They probably have a chil-dren's menu here. So you can order a hamburger. And you can tell the waitress not to let any pineapple or coconut get on your plate.''

''Ti's right, Tim!'' said Sarah-Jane, who also came to the rescue. ''It won't be so terrible. This is the kind of restaurant where you can order a sundae for dessert, and it comes with a little umbrella on it. Right, Aunt Sarah?''

To Timothy's surprise, his mother laughed. ''Your cousins are being very sweet to you, Timothy! Remember, you won't get to see them as much once school starts, so let's make this a nice visit, OK? Let me see you cheer up and be considerate of other people's feelings—the way you usually are.''

Timothy decided this would be a good time to say something uncrabby, so his mother would know he wanted to get back to normal. The problem was, it was hard to sound back to normal when you still weren't feeling like yourself.

But then Timothy thought of something he really wanted to ask about.

# 3
# THE FUNNY-LOOKING STATUE

"Why did the Tropical Gardens restaurant put that monster-thing over there?" Timothy asked. He pointed to the funny-looking statue that stood in the side hallway outside the restaurant.

The six of them walked over to take a closer look at it.

"It's supposed to look like an idol the island people used to worship," explained Timothy's mother. "You learned a commandment about idolatry, remember?"

"The Second Commandment," said Timothy. "The one where it says not to make 'graven images.' A graven image is an idol. So the rule is: 'You shall not make for yourself an idol.'"

Titus said, "Yeah, but the Israelite people kept disobeying that rule. They kept worshiping

things that weren't even God—like a golden calf. I don't understand why they would do that. I mean, how could you *make* something—and then think it could come to life and help you?''

''It doesn't make sense, does it?'' agreed Aunt Jane. ''It's like it says in the psalms: 'The idols of the nations are silver and gold, made by the hands of men. They have mouths, but cannot speak, eyes, but they cannot see; they have ears, but cannot hear, nor is there breath in their mouths.' ''

Sarah-Jane said, ''But do people really *use* this

idol? Do they come here on Sunday and pray to it instead of going to church?''

"No," said Aunt Sue. "This statue is just for decoration. Nowadays when we talk about idols, we mean the modern things people love more than they love God. People can get greedy and put money and other things first. People let other things take charge of their lives instead of God. And that's a kind of idolatry.''

They were all quiet for a while, thinking about that.

Then Timothy's mother said, "Who's hungry? Let's go in.''

Everybody glanced at Timothy to see if he would start complaining again. But he didn't.

# 4
# A CRACK IN THE WALL

Even Timothy had to admit that the restaurant was kind of fun once you got inside. It looked like a native hut, with a straw ceiling and log walls.

"Mom, can we kids have our own booth?" Sarah-Jane begged.

"Oh, I get it," said Aunt Sue. "That way if we moms misbehave, you can pretend like you don't even know us."

"Mo-ther!" said Sarah-Jane. "Be serious!"

"All right," said her mother. "If you three have your own booth, it will give us sisters a chance to talk."

So the three sisters (the moms) sat at one booth, and their three kids (the cousins) sat at another.

The cousins each found something they liked

on the children's menu. And the waitress was very nice when Timothy asked her not to let any pineapple or coconut get on his plate.

Then they each got to order a sundae. Timothy and Titus played with their paper umbrellas a little bit. But then they gave them to Sarah-Jane, who wanted to take them home.

Their mothers still weren't anywhere near finished, so Timothy, Titus, and Sarah-Jane just had to wait.

Timothy could feel himself getting crabby again, and even Sarah-Jane and Titus were getting kind of restless. But then Timothy noticed something interesting.

"Hey, you guys, look at this! This wall has cracks between the logs. And if you put your eye up to the crack, you can see out into the mall!"

Right away, Titus and Sarah-Jane tried it. All three cousins loved mysteries. And peeking through a crack was sort of like detective work.

"Hey, look where we are!" said Sarah-Jane. "We're right behind the idol. It's just on the other side of this wall."

Suddenly the three of them got very quiet,

because something strange was happening out there.

A teenage boy came up to the idol and looked all around. The cousins could see the boy, but he couldn't see them. He thought he was all alone. Quickly he reached into his shirt and pulled out—a big, red artificial flower!

Timothy, Titus, and Sarah-Jane turned to one another in amazement. But they were careful not to make any noise. They watched as the boy ducked down and put his flower among the others around the idol's feet. Then he got up and hurried away.

"What was all that about?" asked Sarah-Jane at last.

"Beats me!" said Titus.

"It's very mysterious!" said Timothy.

# 5

# THE RED FLOWER BUSINESS

When the mothers had finally finished lunch, Aunt Jane said, "Now we have to buy a wedding present for a friend of ours."

"A *wedding* present?" wailed Titus. "You mean *toasters* and junk?"

"Bor-RING!" declared Sarah-Jane.

Timothy grinned. It was nice to hear someone else complaining for a change!

"We knew you'd feel that way," said Aunt Sue. "So maybe you'd like to be on your own while we shop. OK—here are your rules: Stay in the mall. Stay together. And meet us back here in exactly one hour."

The first thing the cousins did when they were on their own was to go around to the side of the restaurant and look at the idol.

It seemed to stare right back at them—but, of course, it couldn't see them. It had little ears—but, of course, it couldn't hear the questions they were asking one another. And it had a wide mouth—but, of course, it couldn't tell them what was going on.

"There's the flower that boy had," said Sarah-Jane, pointing at one.

"How can you tell?" asked Titus.

"Yeah," said Timothy. "There's a zillion flowers there!"

"Because!" said Sarah-Jane. "All the other flowers are *orangey* red. His was *really* red."

"Good thinking, S-J!" said Titus.

"Yes, S-J!" said Timothy. "But it still doesn't explain *why* he put his flower there."

"Maybe it's like a present for the idol?" asked Titus doubtfully. "Maybe that boy really thinks the idol is some kind of god? Maybe he was leaving an offering there?"

"But this idol is just for decoration," said Sarah-Jane. "Maybe he just wanted to add to the decorations?"

The three cousins had to admit they were

stumped. So they went to ride the escalators and think about the red flower some more. When they got to the next level up, they looked down on the idol from above. And it was then that they saw something even stranger.

*Another* teenage boy—a much older one this time—came by and picked up the same red flower. He looked around to make sure no one was watching him, so the cousins ducked down, fast, behind a bench. He fiddled with the flower a little bit, but they couldn't tell what he was doing.

Then he put the flower back—but he didn't put

it back in exactly the same place. This time the red flower went on the *other* side of the idol.

Before the cousins realized what was happening, the boy had disappeared through the outside door that led to the parking lot.

"This is crazy!" said Titus. "*What* is going on?"

Sarah-Jane said, "If you know the red flower is there, you can find it with no trouble. But if you weren't especially looking for it, you wouldn't even notice it."

"But what does it all mean?" asked Timothy. "What makes that one red flower so special? And why are these teenagers picking it up and putting it down?"

As soon as Timothy had said that, they saw the first teenage boy come back again.

And sure enough, he went straight to the same red flower. He picked it up, turned it over, and put it in his pocket. Then he turned and walked quickly away through the mall.

"Will someone *please* tell me what's going on!" said Timothy.

"I wish I knew!" said Sarah-Jane.

"I almost wish idols could talk after all," said Titus. "Then maybe the Tropical Gardens idol could explain this whole business with teenagers and the red flower!"

They sat for a while, watching the idol, but nothing else happened. By that time, they were really tired of scrunching down and needed to stretch their legs.

It wasn't nearly time to meet their mothers yet, so they just wandered up, down, and around the mall.

Timothy got his funny cooped-up feeling again. And the perfume from the candle stores started giving him a headache.

Titus and Sarah-Jane didn't seem to be feeling any better than he was. They had all three seen a mystery happening right in front of their eyes—but they hadn't been able to solve it.

# 6

# THE DETECTIVE GAME

Suddenly Sarah-Jane said, "Hey, Tim! There's your friend Jeff. See him? 'Way up ahead of us."

"Oh, yeah!" said Timothy. But he knew even if he waved and called, he wouldn't be able to get Jeff's attention.

Titus said, "Hey, you guys. I know a kind of detective game we could play. Let's follow Jeff and see how long it takes him to notice us."

It sounded like a fun game, but Timothy wasn't sure he felt like playing anything. But then he remembered that his mother wanted him to be considerate of his cousins' feelings. So he said, "Well, OK. Let's give it a try."

Titus and Sarah-Jane got caught up in the game right away. They started off by arguing about whether they should wear their sunglasses or not.

Sarah-Jane thought sunglasses would make a good disguise. Titus said sunglasses would only make them *more* noticeable, since they'd be the only people wearing shades indoors.

Timothy said, "If you two don't stop arguing, we're going to lose Jeff."

"Oh, no!" said Sarah-Jane. "Forget the sunglasses; let's *go*!"

Jeff was wearing a bright, yellow T-shirt, so it wasn't too hard to keep him in sight. They got as close as they could, weaving in and out of the crowds. They followed him past the waterfall and over the little bridge.

When Jeff turned a corner, the cousins plastered themselves against the wall and peeked around the corner to make sure Jeff wasn't right there—just waiting for them. He wasn't. He was safely up ahead.

Once, though, Jeff looked around as if he were trying to figure out where he was. "Look out, look out, look out," said Titus out of the corner of his mouth. He grabbed a flyer from a rack that said, *Free—Take One* and pretended to read it. Timothy and Sarah-Jane did the same thing.

But Jeff wasn't looking at them. He kept looking nervously at his watch, as if it were almost time for him to be someplace.

Finally Jeff rode down an escalator, and the cousins got on, too. They had been so busy watching Jeff that they hadn't really noticed where they were going. Then suddenly—they found themselves back at the Tropical Gardens restaurant.

By this time, they were close enough to jump out and say "Hi" to Jeff. And they were just about to do that—but something stopped them.

Jeff went to the quiet corner of the mall, to where the idol was. He quickly looked around him.

Without talking it over, the cousins all hid behind a pillar. Then they watched Jeff take a red flower out from under his T-shirt. He placed it by the idol. Then he quickly walked away.

"That does it!" said Timothy. "We have to get to the bottom of this flower business."

Quickly and quietly they ran over to the idol. Timothy snatched up the flower and turned it over in his hands.

"What's that?" asked Titus. He was pointing to a little packet that was taped to the underside of the flower.

"I say we open it and find out," said Timothy. "It belongs to Jeff, and I'm a friend of his. We don't want anybody else to get it."

Titus pulled the packet off the flower. Timothy put the packet in his pocket. And Sarah-Jane carefully put the flower back in place.

Then they scooted across the mall, to a little hallway where the telephones were. They could still see most of the idol, and they figured they were in a pretty good hiding place themselves.

Titus took the phone off the hook and pretended to punch the buttons. "That way it will just look like three kids calling someone," he explained.

"Good idea, Ti," said Sarah-Jane. "Let's just hope no one comes along, who wants to use the phone!"

Timothy's hands were shaking a little bit as he unwrapped the packet.

When he finally got it open, all three of them gasped.

# 7

# AN AWFUL THOUGHT

It was money. All folded up in a tight little square.

"That's weird!" said Titus. "Why would Jeff tape money to a flower?"

"Yeah," said Timothy. "And then why did he go away and leave it?"

"I wonder if the first boy left money on his flower, too?" said Sarah-Jane.

But they didn't have time to talk about that, because they saw the second boy—the older one—again. The three cousins crowded back as far as they could in the telephone hallway. They could still see the idol. And they saw the older boy go to the idol and pick up Jeff's red flower.

Right away he turned it over as if he expected to find something there. But, of course, he didn't, because Timothy still held Jeff's money tightly in his hand.

At first the older boy looked puzzled. Then he looked angry. He threw the flower down and left by the outside door.

Just then someone came along to use the telephone, so the cousins went and sat on a bench in front of the restaurant.

"OK, let's think about this," said Timothy. "Why would some kids leave money for some other kid to find? Maybe they're buying something from him? But what?"

"Something small," said Titus. "Small enough to fit under a big artificial flower."

"Jewels!" said Sarah-Jane. "Maybe that older boy is a jewel thief, and he's selling stolen jewels to the other boys."

Timothy shook his head. "Why would kids want to buy jewels? Besides, I don't think there's enough money here for diamonds and stuff."

Titus said, "Well, maybe the kids paid the older kid to put a bug in the flower."

Sarah-Jane shuddered. "You mean like a *spider*? Ugh! Why would they do that?"

"No, no," said Titus quickly. "I meant one of those little things people use to listen in on other people's conversations. You know—they call it—um—an 'eavesdropping device.' "

Timothy said, "Yeah, but what kind of secret conversations could you hear in a mall? Besides, the bug wasn't in the flower long enough to pick up much of anything. . . . I know! I bet the older boy put *microfilm* under the flower. I bet the microfilm has a list of enemy spies or something on it. The older boy is a *double agent*. And—and the other kids are spies, who are buying *TOP SECRETS* from him!!"

Sarah-Jane frowned doubtfully. "Can teenagers really get jobs as spies?" she asked. "My baby-sitter just works at McDonald's."

Timothy thought about that for a minute. "Yeah, you're right, S-J. I suppose teenagers *could* be spies, but they're probably not."

"OK," said Sarah-Jane. "So let's think some more about teenagers. Ti—what's the matter? You look so white!"

Timothy looked at Titus in alarm when Sarah-Jane said that. He had heard about people turning

pale before, but he'd never really seen it happen.
"What's the matter Ti? You look like you just
thought of something awful."

"I did," said Titus in a small voice. "Drugs."

Timothy and Sarah-Jane stared at him.

Then Timothy said fiercely, "No! No way! Jeff would never do drugs! He's too smart for that! Drugs are like the modern idols and stuff Aunt Sue was talking about. They can take over your life and ruin it. It can't be drugs. Let's think some more!"

But as soon as Titus had said the word, Timothy and Sarah-Jane both knew that he was right.

They were sad—but not really surprised—when Jeff came back and hurried toward the idol. Quickly he picked up his red flower and turned it over. When he saw there was no packet from the older boy—and no money either—he sat right down on the floor across from the idol and put his head in his hands.

He didn't even hear the cousins as they came up beside him.

"Here's your money back," said Timothy.

Jeff jumped up. "Timothy, you little idiot! How did you get mixed up in this? Don't you know how dangerous it is? What are you doing here?"

Timothy didn't answer any of Jeff's questions; he had some questions of his own. "*I'm* not the idiot, Jeff! *You're* the idiot! You were buying drugs, weren't you? Don't you know that's stupid—and wrong?"

By now Timothy was crying, but he didn't care.

"No, Tim, no!" said Jeff. "Listen to me! I don't do drugs—honest, I don't. You've got to believe me! This was the first time I ever even tried to buy them. Some guys I sort of hang around with all got some money together. And then we drew straws to see who would go get the stuff—and—and it turned out to be me."

"Yeah?" said Timothy, swallowing hard and angrily wiping away some tears. "That still doesn't explain why you wanted to try drugs in

the first place!''

Jeff sounded very tired. ''I don't know, Timothy. I thought it would be fun, I guess. I thought it would be cool. And I thought it would help. I've been going through a hard time lately. Having some pretty bad days. . . .''

''So?'' said Timothy. ''Everybody has bad days. *I* do! Are you saying I should use drugs, too?''

Jeff's mouth dropped open, and he stared at Timothy in dismay. ''Don't even *think* that! You're—you're like a little brother to me. I would never, *never* want you to try this!''

"Then why did *you*?" asked Timothy.

Jeff shook his head. "I don't know, kid. But I'm beginning to think it was a really bad idea! Listen—I'm going to give my friends their money back—and tell them to count me out. How's that?" He put his arm around Timothy's shoulders, and Timothy didn't pull away.

Titus and Sarah-Jane glanced at each other. They were glad to hear that Timothy's friend had changed his mind about trying drugs, but there was still a lot they wanted to know.

# 9
# THE T.C.D.C.

"What was all this business with the red flower?" asked Titus.

Jeff sighed. "I don't know. That's just the way this dealer kid likes to work. We heard about it from some guys who buy from him. They put their money under a red flower by that statue thing. Then they have to go away for a while so they don't see him. He comes along and gets the money—and leaves the stuff. Then he moves the flower so you know he's been there. And later you can come back and pick it up.

"I guess he figures that the statue is an easy marker for people to find. And the flowers make a good hiding place. It's kind of dumb and dramatic, but it's how he likes to do things."

"It doesn't matter *how* he does it," said Sarah-

Jane. "He's still greedy and rotten! You should turn him in—or tell his parents—or *something*!"

"I know," said Jeff miserably. "But I don't know who he is. I don't even know what he looks like."

"That's OK," said Titus. "*We* do."

Timothy, Titus, and Sarah-Jane were good detectives, who noticed things. And so they were able to give Jeff a very good description of the dealer kid. And as they talked, they could tell that Jeff realized he knew who the boy was.

"You kids are really on the ball!" Jeff said.

"Well, that's how it is," said Timothy. "You can depend on the T.C.D.C.!"

Jeff looked confused. "What's a 'teesy-deesy'?" he asked.

"It's letters," explained Sarah-Jane.
"Capital T.
Capital C.
Capital D.
Capital C.
It stands for the Three Cousins Detective Club."

Jeff smiled gently. "Well, I'm glad the T.C.D.C. was around! It kept me from doing

42

something really stupid.''

The cousins were so busy talking to Jeff that they didn't hear their mothers come up.

''There you are,'' said Aunt Jane. ''We were waiting for you at the front of the restaurant.''

Timothy's mother looked at him closely. ''Timothy!'' she said. ''Have you been crying? I knew you were having a hard time today, but I didn't know you felt *this* bad!''

Timothy looked at Jeff. Jeff cleared his throat and said, ''Mrs. Dawson, I think I need to explain a few things.''

Much as Timothy, Titus, and Sarah-Jane loved detective work, they were glad to have their mothers take over the problem with Jeff. They talked with him about what a serious situation he'd gotten into. And Timothy's mother said she would help him tell his parents about it.

## 10
## NO COCONUTS!

Timothy was glad to get home and lie in his own yard, where there was no roof over the trees.

"You know what I like about these trees?" Timothy said to Titus and Sarah-Jane. "There are no coconuts growing on them!"

Titus and Sarah-Jane laughed.

"Yes," said Titus. "This is just a nice, ordinary yard. No big, fancy, red flowers!"

"Right!" said Sarah-Jane. "And no funny-looking statues!"

But the best thing about his yard, Timothy decided, was that it was next door to Jeff's. Timothy knew that he wanted to go on being friends with Jeff. And he would even go on pretending, sometimes, that Jeff was his big brother.

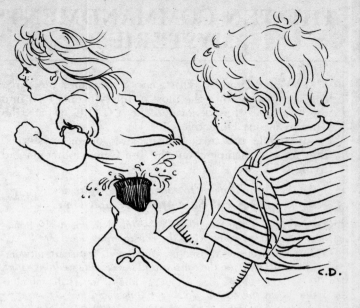

Timothy felt happy all over when he thought about what Jeff had said to him: "You're— you're like a little brother to me."

"What do you guys want to do now?" Timothy asked his cousins.

"I know!" cried Sarah-Jane excitedly. "Why don't we try on our new clothes and play school?"

Timothy filled a cup with water from the garden hose and chased her all the way down the block.

The End

# THE TEN COMMANDMENTS MYSTERIES

When Timothy, Titus, and Sarah-Jane, the three cousins, get together the most ordinary events turn into mysteries. So they've formed the T.C.D.C. (That's the Three Cousins Detective Club.)

And while the three cousins are solving mysteries, they're also learning about the Ten Commandments and living God's way.

### You'll want to solve all ten mysteries along with Sarah-Jane, Ti, and Tim:

The Mystery of the Laughing Cat—"You shall not steal." *Someone stole rare coins. Can the cousins find the thief?*

The Mystery of the Messed-up Wedding—"You shall not commit adultery." *Can the cousins find the missing wedding ring?*

The Mystery of the Gravestone Riddle—"You shall not murder." *Can the cousins solve a 100-year-old murder case?*

The Mystery of the Carousel Horse—"You shall not covet." *Why does the stranger want an old, wooden horse?*

The Mystery of the Vanishing Present—"Remember the Sabbath day and keep it holy." *Can the cousins figure out who has Grandpa's missing birthday gift?*

The Mystery of the Silver Dolphin—"You shall not give false testimony." *Who's telling the truth—and who's lying?*

The Mystery of the Tattletale Parrot—"You shall not misuse the name of the Lord your God." *What will the beautiful green parrot say next?*

The Mystery of the Second Map—"You shall have no other gods before me." *Can the cousins discover who dropped the strange map?*

The Mystery of the Double Trouble—"Honor your father and your mother." *How could Timothy be in two places at once?*

The Mystery of the Silent Idol—"You shall not make for yourself an idol." *If the idol could speak, what would it tell the cousins?*

*Available at your local Christian bookstore.*

David C. Cook Publishing Co., Elgin, IL 60120

# SHOELACES AND BRUSSELS SPROUTS

## One little lie, but BIG trouble!

When Alex lies to her mom about losing her shoelaces, it doesn't seem like a big deal. But how do you replace special baseball laces when you don't have any money and you're not allowed to go to the store alone? A big softball game is coming up, and Alex knows the coach won't let her pitch in shoes without laces—or in cowboy boots!

Every kid gets into the predicaments that Alex does—ones that start out small and mushroom. Readers will learn from Alex's mistakes and understand that they have the same sources of help that she turns to: A God who loves them and wants to help them, and parents who understand.

### Other books in the Alex Series . . .

2 *French Fry Forgiveness*—Sometimes making friends is harder than making enemies.

3 *Hot Chocolate Friendship*—Is winning first place as important to Alex as being a friend?

4 *Peanut Butter and Jelly Secrets*—Obeying her parents (even in little things) beats the awful results of disobeying.

*Available at your local Christian bookstore.*

David C. Cook Publishing Co.
850 N. Grove Ave.
Elgin, IL 60120

**Chariot Books**